MARTIAN MUSTACHE MISCHIEF!

by
Brian (Planet) Rock

Illustrations by
Joshua Dawson

This book is dedicated to ketchup lovers everywhere!

Visit
www.BrianRock.net
to keep up with Brian's latest releases
and new freebies every month!

Published by First Light Publishing

ISBN 13# 978-0-692-51651-5

Have you seen any big, red, furry mustaches running around?

No?

That's good.

What, you don't know about the mustaches? Maybe I should explain...

It all started a few weeks ago. The town astronomer noticed that the planet Mars was losing its red color. Then, three days ago, he noticed some flashes of light on the Martian surface.

What does Mars have to do with mustaches?

EVERYTHING!

Ten tiny Martian spaceships landed outside of town. When the Martians came out, they looked like big, fuzzy caterpillars. Their leader spoke up and said, "Give us all your ketchup!"

Of course everyone in town started laughing.

I mean, how can you take a fuzzy, ketchup-eating, caterpillar-looking Martian seriously?

Everyone in town went back about their business.

But the next day, half the town had mysteriously grown mustaches overnight.

Even some of the women and children!

The newly mustachioed townspeople started acting odd.

They talked in a strange, robot-like tone. They didn't blink their eyes.

They were *always* hungry. And...

they put ketchup on EVERYTHING they ate.

They put ketchup on their cereal. They put ketchup on toast. They put ketchup on their yogurt and bananas and chocolate milk and pizza.

They even smothered their ice cream in ketchup!

The more ketchup they ate, the redder their mustaches got.

Finally, someone figured out what happened.

The Martians attached themselves to people when they were asleep or distracted.

Then, disguised as mustaches, they used *mind control* to make people eat food smothered in ketchup.

Why ketchup?

Because they want to use our ketchup to give Mars back its red color.

If we don't stop them, there'll be no more ketchup left on earth!

That's why we need your help.

Will you help us stop the Martian Mustaches?

Great!

Luckily, our scientists figured out two ways to stop the Martians.

The first way to stop them is to say, "**Martian Mustache Mischief**" three times fast.

(According to our scientists, Martians really hate tongue twisters.)

Let's practice together. Whenever you see a Martian Mustache, say:

Martian Mustache Mischief!
Martian Mustache Mischief!
Martian Mustache Mischief!

Hmmm. Maybe we'd better focus on plan #2.

The second way to get rid of Martian Mustaches is to...

Hey, is that a caterpillar down there?

I am suddenly hungry. Do you have any ketchup?

What's that? Did you say, "Martin must have misfits?" Why are you saying that three times?

I must get food - with ketchup.

Oh look, pancakes!

Please pass the ketchup.

And the pepper. I like pepper.

Oops, I spilled some pe- pe- pe- Atchooo!

And the second way to get rid of Martian Mustaches (in case you have trouble with the tongue twister,) is to make whoever's wearing them sneeze. Usually a little pepper will do the trick.

Hey, where am I?

Where did these pancakes come from?

Oh no! The earthlings have sneezed on us! Run for your lives!

Hooray! You helped us drive out the Martians!

Excuse me, do you have any ketchup?

Get your very own

Martian Mustache cut-out at

www.BrianRock.net

JAN   2017

2 1982 02737 0489

CPSIA information can be obtained
at www.ICGtesting.com
Printed in the USA
LVOW06s1435120117
520747LV00023B/267/P